STALKED BY THE BODYGUARD

EMMA BRAY

PROLOGUE

Willow

THE BLARING horns and revving engines envelop me as I step onto the crowded sidewalk. This is Los Angeles in all its chaotic glory. I smooth down my floral sundress, taking a deep breath. My name is Willow Carter and this city is my kingdom.

I catch a glimpse of my reflection in a storefront window, my long blonde curls framing my face, green eyes bright with anticipation. I've learned to keep my guard up in this town. You never know who might be watching.

A sleek black car slows beside me, the tinted window rolling down. I freeze, poised for flight.

"Hey there gorgeous, need a ride?" The driver leers at me hungrily.

I square my shoulders and walk on. "No thanks, I'm good."

The car keeps pace with me. "Come on baby, I'll show you a real good time."

My skin crawls at his words. I spin to face him, anger simmering in my veins. "I said no. Now leave me the hell alone."

The driver's expression darkens. For a moment we're locked in a standoff, the rumbling car engine the only sound. Then he peels away, nearly clipping my leg.

I watch the car until it disappears, willing my pounding heart to slow. I hate how weak they make me feel, like a lamb among wolves. But this lamb has teeth. And she's not afraid to bite.

I take a deep breath and center myself, brushing off the encounter. I can't let creeps like him ruin my day. Today is important. I have a big audition that could change everything.

Music is my passion. Ever since I was a little girl, singing has been my escape, my salvation. Now at nineteen, it's finally my career. I've paid my dues playing dive bars and coffee shops, hoping for my big break.

And today might just be it.

I arrive at the prestigious recording studio, heart

fluttering with nerves and excitement. This is my shot to impress a major producer and land a record deal.

The receptionist leads me to the studio where a team waits—manager, vocal coach, producer. The producer, Dante, rises to shake my hand.

"Willow, so glad you could make it. We've heard great things about your voice."

I smile, willing my nerves away. "Thank you. I'm thrilled to be here."

We get to work on a new song they've written for me. As the music starts, the familiar thrill rushes through me. This is what I live for. I close my eyes, let the melody fill me up, and begin to sing...

The hours fly by in a blur of takes and notes. When we finish, Dante grins and claps. "Incredible! You have real star power, Willow. How would you like to make an album with us?"

Joy surges within me. My dreams are finally coming true. "I'd love nothing more," I say.

This is only the beginning. With music as my wings, there's no telling how far I'll fly.

CHAPTER
ONE

Willow

BUT WITH SUCCESS COMES DARKNESS.

The album is a smash hit, my name and face suddenly everywhere. I'm stopped constantly on the street, photographed without consent. My social media is flooded with messages from obsessed fans, some worrisome in their intensity.

My team insists this is normal, but their reassurances ring hollow. I feel exposed, hunted. My blossoming fame has placed a target on my back.

I take precautions. Vary my routine, keep my head down. My guard is always up, eyes sweeping my surroundings. I check the locks twice at night, sleep with a bat by my bed. I'm almost afraid to be in public alone.

But still, the paranoia grows. I'm jumpy. I avoid people, cutting off friends and family. It's safer to be alone.

The darkness closes in, strangling my spirit. This is the cost of living my dream—a loss of freedom, of self. Each achievement only tightens the vise.

But the show must go on. I straighten my shoulders and descend into the flashing lights. For the roar of the crowd, I silence the screams within.

———

The shrill beep of my alarm jolts me awake. 5:30 AM. Time to start another day in the life of Willow Carter, pop star extraordinaire.

I drag myself out of bed with a groan. My body aches, still exhausted from last night's sold-out show. No rest for the weary.

After a quick shower, I throw on leggings and a hoodie, twisting my damp hair into a bun. A light breakfast—oatmeal and fruit— and then it's time for vocals.

I arrive at the studio by seven. I'm greeted by my producer, Chad. We jump right into warmups and run through a few tracks. My voice is still raspy, but a honey lemon tea helps soothe my throat.

Chad pushes me hard, demanding take after take

until I nail the high notes. "C'mon Willow, I know you got more in you!" It's exhausting, but it brings out my best.

By noon, I'm starving. My assistant brings takeout salads to the studio. We review tour logistics over lunch—venues booked, rehearsals scheduled. It never stops.

After lunch is media training. My publicist, Amanda, grills me on interview questions. "Don't reveal too much personal info. Keep it light." I plaster on my media smile and rattle off practiced answers.

Finally, I hit the gym at 4 PM. A tough workout with my trainer to stay tour-ready. Every muscle burns by the end.

At home, I heat up a frozen meal and video chat my little sister. It's a bright spot in my day, though too short.

By 9 PM, I'm spent. But sleep won't come easy. My mind spins with lyrics, melodies, endless to-do lists. The machine never sleeps, and neither can I.

Another day on the hamster wheel of fame. It's a relentless grind, but I live for the thrill of creating music. For those moments lost in the flow of singing, I push through the exhaustion. This is the life I chose. No regrets.

———

The streets of LA blur past as I stare out the tinted window of the black SUV. Bright lights, honking horns, the constant hum of the city that never sleeps. But something feels off tonight. The energy changed when I left the studio.

I press my forehead to the glass, eyes darting between buildings, searching for I don't know what. My gut twists. We stop at a red light, and I scan the sidewalks. Look for anything out of place, anyone paying too much attention. My fans are always enthusiastic but mostly harmless. Most days I revel in their adoration, but lately...

"You okay, Miss Carter?" my driver asks, eyes flicking to the rearview mirror.

"Yeah, fine," I mutter.

We pull into the underground garage of my highrise. I wait, poised, as the driver opens the door. Sunglasses on, head down, move quick—the usual routine.

In the elevator, I feel caged. I jab the button for my floor. *Come on, come on.* The doors slide open and I power walk to my door, keys clutched like a weapon.

Inside, I engage the three locks and lean against the door, pulse racing.

Get it together, Willow. You're being paranoid.

But I can't escape the creeping dread that something is coming for me.

I pour a glass of wine with shaky hands. I'm technically too young to legally drink, but with fame comes perks. I can get anything I want.

I turn up the stereo to drown out my thoughts. Tomorrow I'll call my manager again and push for more security.

But will it ever be enough?

Fame and fear. Two sides of my tangled life. I gulp the wine, craving the numbness it brings.

But beneath the haze, the shadows still lurk, waiting to consume me.

CHAPTER
TWO

Maverick

THE SPOTLIGHT HITS and the roar of the crowd fills my ears. My eyes lock on Willow as she takes the stage, her blonde curls bouncing with each step. Even from my perch backstage, her magnetism draws me in. I swallow. This girl is enchanting—she commands every room she enters.

My phone buzzes in my pocket, snapping me back. It's a text from Willow's manager:

> Remember, not a word to her about you. We need to keep her safe.

I slip the phone away, refocusing on the mission.

Willow grabs the mic, flashing a smile that sparks a pang deep in my core. Her voice is honey, sweet and smooth, yet with a raspiness that keeps me leaning in. This job just got a lot more complicated. Every word from her lips stirs something primal in me that I can't shake. I'm supposed to protect this siren, but I'm the one in danger of being lured onto the rocks by her spell.

I melt into the shadows as she works the stage. Her talent is raw, almost feral, unlike anything I've ever seen. She becomes the music, each note possessing her. I understand now why she needs protection—a creature this exquisite will have enemies lurking in the darkness.

I will keep her safe, I vow to myself. *No harm will come to her as long as I'm here.*

But there's a new threat, one I couldn't have predicted. My own desire clouds my judgement and makes me weak. I cannot fall prey to it. I must remain vigilant for any dangers to her—even if that danger is myself.

———

Her voice cascades through the smoky club, husky and sensual. She's a siren calling to me, her spell sinking into my bones. *Focus*, I tell myself, dragging my gaze from her hypnotic sway. I'm here to protect—not leer like a smitten schoolboy.

She moves with such grace, bare feet caressing the stage as if it were a lover beneath her. I imagine those feet on me, my body her stage, and clench my fists.

Get it together, McKenzie.

When she dances, it's liquid fire. Each gyration of her hips stokes the flames building inside me. A sheen of sweat on her skin makes her glow under the stage lights. I want to run my tongue along that sweet, salty glaze.

Down boy, I silently warn my traitorous body. She's a job, not a conquest. But God, just look at her. Those plush lips I want to crush with my own. Satin hair I ache to twist around my fist. And those eyes. Emeralds flashing as the music takes her higher, to a place beyond my reach.

I'm losing myself in her. The very thing I swore wouldn't happen. But she's in my blood now, this siren song I cannot resist. I'll protect her from the dangers that lurk in the shadows and keep her light burning bright.

But who will protect her from me?

The final chord rings out and Willow collapses onto the empty stage, chest heaving. I want to run to her, scoop her limp body into my arms. Instead, I melt into the shadows as the crowd roars.

She rises slowly, a triumphant smile lighting up her face. Her eyes scan the darkness beyond the stage, searching. Does she sense me here? My heart thrums an eager beat.

I slip outside and wait by the stage door, needing to see her up close. Needing her to see me. She emerges flanked by her entourage.

I try to ignore the pang in my chest when she doesn't even glance my way because that's as it should be. She shouldn't notice me.

I'm just paid to protect her in silence.

———

Her schedule becomes my schedule. I shadow her every move—from sleepy morning coffee to late night showers. I catalog every detail. The way she tosses her hair over one shoulder when she laughs. The scent of her shampoo as she brushes by.

At first, it was for her safety. To scan for threats, identify risks. But now, I admit, it's become more. An obsession. A need to know her. Consume her.

I crave her nearness like a drug, finding excuses to hover in doorways as she changes clothes. To accompany her on mundane errands just to inhale her sweet perfume.

At night I lie awake, imagining the soft curves

hidden beneath her clothes. The warmth of her bare skin against mine. I jack off until I come harder than I've ever come in my life.

But it's not enough. I want *her*.

I've never wanted anyone this intensely. It scares me. And thrills me.

But I resist. Barely. My desire is a wild thing straining against a fragile leash. If I unleashed it, the fallout could be catastrophic. For both of us.

So, I watch. And *want*. Playing a twisted game of temptation I'm destined to lose. She doesn't know the power she wields over me. That with one whispered word, she could shatter my control.

For now, I remain the protector. But soon, God help me, I'll be the predator too. And once that side of me emerges, there will be no going back.

She'll be mine. In every way imaginable. And I will show no mercy.

I take a deep breath, trying to clear my mind as I watch Willow from the shadows. She's radiant under the stage lights, her voice soaring through the speakers, captivating the crowd. This is where she belongs, I remind myself. In the spotlight, shining for the world to see.

Not pressed against me in the darkness, those lips parted in ecstasy, green eyes clouded with desire...

I grit my teeth, cursing inwardly at the images that invade my thoughts. This obsession is getting out of hand. I'm her protector, not her lover. No matter how fiercely my body burns for her.

The show ends and the crowd erupts in applause. Willow beams, blowing kisses. My heart constricts. Does she have any idea what she does to me? How she makes me ache?

I fight the urge to go to her as she heads backstage. To pull her into my arms and—

No. I force myself to turn away. She is not mine to take. I repeat the words like a mantra, clinging to the last frayed threads of my restraint.

Soon she will be whisked away by her entourage, and I will resume my watch from afar. For now, the battle is won. But my desire continues to grow, an obsession I can no longer control.

She will be mine, I vow silently. No matter the cost. I will find a way to make her see we belong together. And once I have her, I will *never* let her go.

CHAPTER
THREE

Willow

THE ROAR of the crowd still rings in my ears as I make my way backstage, the adrenaline from the performance coursing through my veins. Roadies and techs rush by, coiling wires and packing up equipment in a whirlwind of controlled chaos. I'm floating, drunk on the high that only a flawless set can bring. This is my element. The stage is my home.

Out of the corner of my eye, I catch a shadow detaching itself from the wall. A tall, broad-shouldered figure emerges, eyes intent on my every move. I suppress a shiver as those dark eyes track me through the maze of rigging and amps. He moves with a lethal grace, his muscular frame coiled and ready for action. Predatory. Possessive. He wants to consume me whole.

I quicken my pace, unnerved by the intensity of his gaze, my heels clicking sharply on the concrete floor. I can feel him drawing closer, his presence looming at my back. My heart pounds against my ribs. Who is this man that watches me like forbidden fruit, ripe for the taking? His aura drips with danger, desire, the promise of ruin. I dare not turn, refusing to meet the fire in those fathomless eyes. He would swallow me alive and I would let him.

I round a corner, lost in my own head, and collide with a solid wall of muscle. Strong hands grasp my arms, steadying me before I can fall. My breath catches as I find myself drowning in dark, smoldering eyes, those same eyes I'm running from. How did he move so quickly? Those eyes pierce my soul, laying me bare. His sensual lips curl into a knowing smile.

"We meet at last, Willow," he purrs, his voice a low caress.

I suppress a shiver at the sound of my name on his lips. He straightens, hands still gripping my arms with possessive pressure. Power radiates from his imposing frame. My mouth goes dry.

"I'm Maverick," he says. "Your new bodyguard."

The words send a jolt through me. Bodyguard? I try to pull away, but his hands tighten, keeping me caged against him. His eyes blaze with authority, demanding my obedience.

"Time to go home, little songbird."

Maverick tucks my arm in his and steers me through the chaos, our steps falling into sync. My skin tingles everywhere we touch. I chance a glance at his stern profile and wonder if I've just made a deal with the devil himself. But perhaps damnation isn't the worst fate, so long as those lethal arms remain around me.

My breath catches as Maverick's strong arm encircles my waist, guiding me through the pulsing crowd. I'm hyperaware of Maverick's muscular frame pressed against my side, his commanding presence enveloping me.

"This way, little songbird," he murmurs, his warm breath caressing my ear.

A tremor runs through my body at the intimacy of his touch. I glances up at him, taking in his chiseled jaw and intense gaze focused ahead. He exudes an aura of leashed power, of danger barely contained beneath the surface.

My earlier bravado melts away, replaced by uncertainty. I don't know this man who's been tasked with guarding my life. Can I trust him? Allow myself to be so vulnerable?

Sensing my tension, Maverick looks down, obsidian eyes boring into mine. "You have nothing to fear from me," he says softly.

I shiver at the sincerity in his voice. I don't know why, but...I trust him. Something in his eyes tells me he'd never hurt me, that he truly is here to protect me.

I relax and lean into him, the clean scent of his skin enveloping ,my senses. For now, I decide to let my doubts go. To place my faith in this enigmatic protector fate has delivered to my doorstep.

We step out into the cool night air, the din of the crowd fading behind us. Maverick's arm tightens around my waist as he guides me home, our steps falling into an easy rhythm.

And I can't shake the feeling I'm exactly where I belong.

We walk in silence for a while before Maverick takes it upon himself to break the ice.

"So, little songbird, tell me about yourself," Maverick says, his voice a low rumble.

I glance up at him shyly. "What do you want to know?"

His lips quirk up. "Everything."

A nervous flutter stirs in my belly at the intensity of his gaze. "Well, I'm nineteen, and I've been singing since I could talk. Music is my entire world. When I'm on stage, connecting with the audience, it's like nothing else exists."

I pause, surprised at how freely the words are flowing. There's something about Maverick that makes me want to open up, to bare the deepest parts of myself.

"Being a musician...it's who I am. All I've ever dreamed about is sharing my voice with the world. Writing songs that speak to people, that help them feel less alone. That's my purpose."

I trail off, suddenly self-conscious. Maverick is watching me closely, black eyes glinting.

"Don't stop," he murmurs. "It's captivating listening to you talk about your passion. You light up from the inside."

Heat rises in my cheeks at the compliment. I duck my head, hiding a smile. Maybe, just maybe, I've found someone who understands me. Who I can trust after all.

"What about you?" I ask, realizing I know next to nothing about the man assigned to protect me. "How did you become a bodyguard?"

Maverick hesitates, his jaw tightening. I sense I've hit on a sensitive topic.

"Let's just say I've got a very specific skillset," he finally says. "I spent years in special ops, taking on the most dangerous assignments. Seen things that would give most people nightmares."

His eyes cloud over, and he stares off into the distance. I shiver at the darkness in his tone, the violence simmering beneath the surface. This is a man intimately acquainted with death.

"When I got out, bodyguard work seemed the natural transition," he continues quietly. "I'm used to operating in the shadows, neutralizing threats before they materialize. Keeping high profile clients safe is what I was made for."

He levels his gaze at me, and I swallow hard. There's an undercurrent of leashed power radiating from him that makes my pulse skitter.

"I'll keep you safe, Willow. No matter what it takes."

His words resonate through me, equal parts reassuring and frightening. I know without a doubt Maverick will lay down his life for mine. And that absolute loyalty both thrills and terrifies me to my core.

I'm momentarily speechless, processing the grim reality behind Maverick's words. He notices my unease and clears his throat, changing the subject.

"So, tell me about this new album of yours. What's the inspiration behind it?"

I perk up, my passion for music rushing back.

"Well, it's a bit of a departure from my last one. I wanted to explore darker themes, channel my inner turmoil into the lyrics and melodies. There's heartbreak, anger, longing...I poured all my raw emotions into the songs."

I glance at him shyly. "I know. It's not very pop princess of me. But I needed the catharsis. Music is cheaper than therapy, right?"

Maverick smiles, the first unguarded expression I've seen from him.

"I think it's brave to put your true self out there like that. Takes guts to be that vulnerable."

His praise warms me. We chat enthusiastically about favorite artists and songs, discovering mutual loves for moody ballads and soaring anthems. As we near my apartment, I find myself wishing the walk could go on longer.

When we arrive at my door, Maverick turns to face me. The air between us seems to shimmer with possibility.

"Goodnight, Willow," he says softly.

"Goodnight, Maverick."

Our eyes lock, a charged silence stretching between us. Maverick takes a step closer, his hand coming up to cup my cheek.

"Be careful, little songbird," he murmurs. "The world can be a dangerous place."

I swallow, feeling the heat of his hand against my skin. My heart races as I lean into his touch.

"I will," I whisper. "As long as you're here to protect me."

He looks at me for a long moment, and I feel like he's seeing straight through me. Then he nods, his expression unreadable.

"I'll be here," he promises, before turning and disappearing into the night.

I'm left standing there, heart racing, wondering what just happened.

Because I realize I'm not just safe with Maverick.

I'm dangerously attracted to him.

CHAPTER FOUR

Willow

THE ROAR of the crowd pulses through my veins as I stare at my reflection in the dressing room mirror. I smooth my hands over the sequined fabric of my dress, the crystals catching the light. This is it. My moment.

Lost in thought, I don't notice the huge wall of muscle until I collide with his solid frame.

Maverick.

I stumble, arms flailing, but his strong hands grasp my shoulders, steadying me. Our eyes meet for a heated instant before he steps back.

"Sorry," I breathe, cheeks flaming. His stern expression softens.

"Break a leg," he says simply, and I feel the weight of his gaze on me as I hurry past, heart racing. The stage calls, but part of me wishes I could stay here in the charged air between us. Ever since that first night I met him, my thoughts continually stray to him.

When I'm taking a shower...

When I'm alone in my bed at night...

And then I begin to ache between my legs...it's like nothing I've ever felt before. My cheeks flame just thinking about it.

Focus, Willow.

The lights dim, and the energy of the crowd washes over me as I step onto the dark stage. This is my element. I close my eyes and soak in the moment, letting the music flow through me.

"Hello, Cleveland!" I shout into the mic as the stage explodes in light. The audience roars.

My band kicks in with the opening chords of my first song, and I grip the mic, pouring my heart into the lyrics. The music takes me higher, transporting me away from everything else.

I'm breathless by the end of the first number, adrenaline and endorphins flooding my system. I scan the wings and find Maverick watching me, arms crossed over his broad chest. Our eyes connect for a heated instant before I'm pulled back into the show.

Later, I prowl the edge of the stage, mic in hand.

The crowd surges forward, hands outstretched. I reach out too, brushing eager fingertips with my own.

A hand clamps down on my wrist, firm and unyielding. My heart lurches as I'm pulled back from the edge. Maverick's stormy eyes bore into mine, his jaw tight.

"Careful," he warns under his breath.

I swallow and nod. His hand lingers a moment too long before dropping away. I turn back to the audience, hiding my flushed cheeks.

The show ends on a high note, the applause thundering in my ears. I exit the stage, exhilarated. He waits in the wings, watching me with that intense gaze.

The backstage area is a flurry of activity as the crew begins breaking down the set. I linger in the wings, not quite ready to leave the magic of the stage behind.

Maverick stays close, ever vigilant. I find comfort in his solid presence at my back. We stand in easy silence as the noise dies down around us.

Finally, I turn to him, curiosity getting the better of me. "Do you enjoy this? The concerts, I mean."

He considers the question. "It has its...perks." His eyes flick to me, then away.

I flush under his gaze, my skin tingling. The air between us seems charged with possibility. I sway closer, drawn by his magnetism.

Maverick tenses, as if fighting some internal battle.

His hand comes up and then brushes ever so lightly against my cheek. I fight the urge to nuzzle into his hand like a contented kitten.

But then his hand drops from my skin, and my eyes snap open.

His touch lingers on my cheek, sending little sparks dancing across my skin.

Our eyes lock, and in his stern gaze I glimpse a flicker of tenderness. It vanishes as quickly as it appeared, but the damage is done. My heart flutters wildly in my chest like a caged bird.

Maverick steps back, a faint tinge of color on his cheeks. "My apologies, Ms. Carter. That was unprofessional of me."

His gruff tone does little to mask the emotion in his eyes. I know I should look away, but I'm transfixed. "It's okay," I whisper.

An awkward silence falls between us. I'm painfully aware of Maverick's imposing presence, his muscular frame radiating an aura of quiet strength. He could crush me without a second thought, yet I've never felt safer than when I'm with him.

Maverick clears his throat, glancing away. "We should go."

I nod mutely, smoothing my dress with trembling hands. As we walk side by side from the stage, the ghost of his touch still burns on my skin. I can't shake the sense that everything has changed between us. The attraction simmering beneath the surface is now undeniable. Maverick's steely composure seems to be slipping, and I'm terrified to discover what lies underneath.

CHAPTER
FIVE

Maverick

I SHADOW Willow's every step, my eyes tracing the curve of her hips as she sways down the hall. This job will be the death of me.

She breezes into the studio, blonde curls bouncing. My eyes track her every movement, cataloging potential threats. None so far, but I won't relax my vigilance for a moment.

"Maverick, you're hovering," Willow says over her shoulder.

"It's my job to hover," I reply.

She turns and gifts me with a dazzling smile that

makes my heart skip. *Focus*, I remind myself. I'm here to protect her, nothing more.

In the studio, Willow chats with the sound engineer as they get set up for today's recording session. I stand against the wall, arms folded, observing.

"Could you grab me a water?" Willow asks.

I comply, handing her the bottle. Our fingers brush and a spark shoots up my arm. Willow doesn't seem to notice.

"Thanks, Maverick. You're the best."

I give a curt nod, ignoring the way my pulse quickens at her praise.

The session begins, and I watch Willow transform as the music takes over. Here, wrapped in the blanket of a melody, she loses her naive innocence. Her voice pours out smoky and sultry, imbued with a passion that grips me in its clutches.

This is the Willow I crave but cannot have. The one who ignites an all-consuming desire I constantly quell. For her safety, I must maintain distance.

But oh, how I yearn to cross that line.

When the last note fades, Willow beams at me. "What did you think?"

"It was perfect," I reply.

And so are you.

But of course I don't voice that last thought.

Instead, I escort Willow back to her apartment after

the recording session, hyperaware of her proximity. She chatters on about the song while I scan the surroundings, ever vigilant.

As always, I make her wait in the car while I survey the surroundings before letting her out.

And it's a good thing too because at her door, a package waits. I pick it up, noting the lack of return address with unease. Inside, I find a disturbing letter and black rose. My jaw tightens. Not again.

This is the third gift like this I've intercepted in recent weeks, each more unsettling than the last. I haven't told Willow about them. She's seemed more carefree with me around, and I don't want to shatter that.

But this has gone too far. Someone is targeting her, and I need to find out who.

After securing the apartment, I leave Willow with a promise to return early tomorrow. I have plenty of men stationed outside her door. Hell, most of the time I sit outside it myself, but I've got research to do. I've got to get to the bottom of this.

Back in my spartan home, I add the package to a growing collection of disturbing deliveries. I'll find whoever is behind this if it's the last thing I do.

No one threatens Willow on my watch.

CHAPTER
SIX

Maverick

THE SHADOWS SEEM to reach for me as I step into the dimly lit lounge. My eyes scan the room, searching for any sign of a threat, but all I see are the hazy silhouettes of patrons immersed in quiet conversations. This is the meeting place he requested, and my senses are on high alert.

He thinks I don't know who he is, but I do. I'm good at my job. His name is Vincent Barnes. That's about all I've dug up so far with a bit of DNA I gathered from one of his "gifts," but I'll found out more.

Poor Willow is currently unaware of what's going on. There was no way I was actually going to let her receive one of his sick envelopes depicting the vile things he wants to do to her. My hands ball into fists just remembering the last one he sent.

My eyes finally fall on an envelope sitting on a dimly lit table. I open it, and my blood turns to ice.

It's Willow. Candid shots of her going about her daily life, completely unaware she's being watched. The final photo is her bedroom window at night, curtain open, silhouette visible.

Granted, all of these were taken before I was brought in to guard her, but still. Just the thought that he's been watching her all this time. It makes my blood boil.

My heart pounds with impotent fury as I look around the empty lounge. I've dealt with monsters before, but none like Vincent Barnes.

He's toying with me now. Taunting me with these photos.

This is only the beginning. I can feel it. And I know one thing for certain—I'll do whatever it takes to stop him and keep Willow safe, no matter the cost. For her, I'd burn the whole world down.

———

I find Willow in her dressing room, preparing for the show. She's humming softly, lost in her own world, as she arranges her golden curls in the mirror. So innocent. So unaware of the danger that lurks, waiting to strike.

My gut twists. How can I tell her?

"Hey," I say softly from the doorway.

She turns, her face lighting up when she sees me. "Maverick! I didn't hear you come in."

I force a smile, moving to perch on the edge of her vanity table. My fingers brush hers lightly. "How's my girl doing? Ready to wow the crowd tonight?"

Her eyes cloud with uncertainty. She knows me too well. "What's wrong?"

I hesitate. Do I tell her everything and shatter the illusion of safety she so desperately clings to now that she has me as her bodyguard? Or do I shield her from the harsh realities closing in around us?

I opt for a half-truth. "Just some crazy fan mail. Don't worry about it."

She frowns. "What kind of fan mail?"

"It's not a big deal." I squeeze her hand reassuringly. "I'll take care of it. I just need you to be extra careful, okay? No going anywhere alone for now."

Fear flickers across her face. "Maverick, you're scaring me. What's going on?"

I sigh. "It's going to be okay. I promise. I won't let anyone hurt you."

She trembles, and my chest aches. My strong, vibrant Willow, so small and fragile now.

And that infuriates me. Barnes wants a war? He's got one. And I won't stop until Willow is safe once more.

Willow takes a step toward me and searches my face with those piercing green eyes of hers, those eyes that haunt my dreams every night and leave me aching with a permanent hard-on. "Tell me the truth, Maverick. Please."

I hesitate, then decide she needs to know. "Someone's been sending threatening messages. Gifts too—dead flowers, torn up photos of you. It's clear the intent is to frighten you."

Her face pales. "Who would do something like that? Why me?"

"I don't everything yet, but I intend to find out." I cup her cheek. I'm breaking every rule I made. No touching the clients. No getting too close. No telling the clients more than they need to know.

But this is Willow, and I can't help myself. All my rules go out the window when it comes to her. I tell Willow everything I do know about the situation because I feel like she deserves to hear it, and I know she'd want to.

She sits stoically, her face pale as I finish my delivery and rush to reassure her, "Willow, listen to me. I know you're scared, but I promise I will keep you safe. No one is getting near you."

She blinks back tears. "I don't understand. I've never done anything to anyone. All I want is to bring people happiness through my music"

"Hey," I tilt her chin up. "This changes nothing. Don't let some psycho frighten you away from living your dream. You're stronger than that."

Willow nods, a spark of determination in her eyes. "You're right. I can't let this stop me. Fuck Vincent Barnes."

"That's my girl." I smile. "Now go out there and show them what you're made of."

She grins and pulls me in for a fierce hug. I'm shocked, but there's no way in hell I'm going to turn down this opportunity. I wrap my arms around her tiny form and marvel at just how perfect she feels in my arms.

And as I hold her, inhaling the sweet scent of her hair, a surge of protectiveness washes over me. I've never felt this way about a client before.

But Willow isn't just a client. And I'll be damned if I let anyone lay a hand on her.

———

After I've seen Willow safely to her room and make sure plenty of men are stationed outside it, I retreat to my office, closing the door firmly behind me. Time to get to work.

I boot up my computer and pull up the files on this "Vincent Barnes." There's precious little to go on—no employment records, address history, or family ties that I can find. It's as if this man appeared out of thin air.

Leaning back in my chair, I rub my temples. Who is this ghost? And what does he want with Willow?

I flip through the photographs and disturbing "gifts" he's sent. Each item radiates menace, meant to terrorize and intimidate. Vincent wants power over her. He craves control.

A hard knot forms in my gut. I've seen this before with obsessed fans—the ones who believe they "own" the object of their affection. Willow is in real danger.

Outside my office, I hear her sweet voice trilling out a new song during rehearsal. The melodic tones contrast sharply with the dark thoughts occupying my mind. I have to end this threat before it steals that light from her forever.

Picking up my phone, I start calling in favors from old contacts. Someone out there knows this Vincent Barnes. And I'm going to dig up every scrap of dirt on him until I find a way to stop him for good. Willow's counting on me.

The shadows grow long as afternoon fades to dusk.

An ominous weight presses down on me. But I won't rest until Willow is safe. I made her a promise—one I intend to keep, no matter what secrets lurk in Vincent's past. She will not become another victim. Not on my watch.

CHAPTER
SEVEN

Willow

I GLANCE out the window of my apartment, wary of any movement in the darkening streets below. Ever since the first disturbing letter arrived, my world has shrunk.

My days are consumed with watching over my shoulder, starting at unexpected sounds. I've stopped my morning runs, canceled appearances, changed my number. But nothing feels safe anymore.

At night, I toss and turn, imagining his cold eyes watching me. What does Vincent Barnes want? Why has he fixated on me?

Exhausted, I sink onto the couch next to Maverick.

He's been my rock through this nightmare. I don't know what I'd do without him right now.

"Maverick, be honest. Do you think he'll actually try to hurt me?" My voice wavers.

Maverick's jaw tightens, his expression grim. "I won't let that happen. We're going to find him and put a stop to this."

"But how? The police keep saying there's nothing they can do until he actually approaches me. I feel so powerless just waiting for that to happen."

Maverick turns to face me, his eyes burning with intensity. "I promise you, Willow, I'm handling this. I've got every resource on it. No one is going to get near you."

I search his face and see the truth there. Maverick won't let me down. For the first time in weeks, a spark of hope flickers inside me.

I cling to that hope as I get ready for bed, Maverick stationed just outside my room as always. Sliding under the covers, I will my racing mind to quiet.

But then I hear a sharp crack on the window and scream.

Maverick is in the room in half a second. He instantly runs to the window to check everything out as he radios his team outside. Once he gets the all clear, I see his big shoulders relax as he turns to me.

I'm still huddled in the bed sitting up with the

covers pulled up to my chin in terror like a ridiculous little girl when Maverick slowly crosses the room toward me.

"It's okay, Willow," he tells me gently. It was just a branch hitting the window.

My shoulders slump in relief, and then a wave of embarrassment washes over me. I drop my face into my hands and begin to cry, all the stress and anxiety of the past few weeks finally coming out.

Maverick sits on the edge of the bed uncertainly, and then I don't know what comes over me, but I throw myself into his arms.

He catches me, and I climb into his lap so that I'm straddling him. I burrow my face into his chest and cry, taking comfort in how safe I feel with his big arms wrapped around me. I deeply breathe in his sandal-wood scent and let it comfort me.

He strokes his hands over my hair soothingly and whispers soothing words to me. "It's okay. I've got you, little songbird."

Little songbird. I love how he calls me that. And I love it when he calls me his girl. I know he might not mean it the way it sounds, but I am.

I'm his.

"Stay with me tonight, Maverick."

Maverick goes completely still, but I press on. "*Please.* Please don't leave me alone."

His eyes darken, conflict playing across his rugged features. I know this crosses the line of duty, but in this moment nothing else matters but the heat coursing between us.

He's quiet for a moment before he finally whispers in a ragged voice. "I'll never leave you alone, Willow. I'll always be here to protect you."

I reach up, tangling my fingers in his hair, and pull his mouth down to mine. I don't know what I'm doing. I'm just following some instinct that's guiding me.

His lips are firm yet gentle as he returns my kiss. He groans, and I can feel his hands trembling against my back as he pulls me closer and deepens the kiss, our tongues dancing in reckless desire.

My skin tingles everywhere his hands explore. I cling to him, craving more of his touch, his taste, his scent.

A pounding ache builds in my core as he trails kisses down my neck.

"Maverick," I whisper, and it's a plea and a prayer all at once.

He grinds against me, and I feel how hard he is, ready for me.

"Willow," he groans as he gives me a look that's a cross between a growl and a tortured plea.

He slides his hands along my thighs, and the ache inside flares into full-blown need.

I claw at the buttons of his shirt, desperate to feel his heated skin against my hands. When I finally get the shirt open, I run my hands over his hard chest and marvel at how strong he is.

He begins kissing my neck, sending delicious shivers down my spine. He sucks on my sensitive skin, and I let out a soft moan. My fingers find the button of his jeans, and I quickly undo it.

I slide down to his hips and slip his pants off, followed by his boxer briefs. I start to climb back up him, but he stops me.

I look up at his questioningly, and then let out a squeal as he picks me up and flips me onto my back. Before I know it, he's got me pinned beneath him, his strong, muscular body barely allowing me room to breathe. His eyes burn into me, and he gently brushes his lips against mine.

I stare back at him, at this gorgeous, broken man who's so much more than he seems. I feel like he sees into my soul.

"Fuck, my little songbird," he whispers, and then his lips are on me again.

His tongue presses against mine, and he tastes like destiny. I want to feel him against me, everywhere. I want to taste his skin and memorize it. I want to drown in his touch like I'm drowning in this unnamed desire that's consuming me.

We break away for the briefest moment. He stares down into my eyes, and I'm drowning in the darkness of his gaze. It's a storm of desire and a hurricane of passion. I've been tossed into that swirling storm, and I'm not sure I'll ever be the same again.

"Maverick," I breathe.

He kisses me again before I can say another word. This time his kiss is painful, like he's giving himself over to the storm that's raging inside. The kiss is raw and hungry.

He trails hot kisses down my neck and across my collarbone, before he pulls the cup of my bra down and sucks my nipple into his mouth. I gasp, surprised by the sensation. His tongue swirls around my hard, sensitive flesh, and the ache in my core grows unbearable.

He slides one hand from my thigh up to my bottom, and then cups me firmly before running his thumb across my core.

I moan as his touch sends waves of pleasure rippling through my body.

He pushes my shirt up around my hips, and I let out a soft gasp as he hooks his fingers into the sides of my panties, and then he tugs. In one swift motion, I'm completely naked beneath him.

I've never felt so open, so exposed.

"You've got a beautiful body, my songbird," he

whispers, moving his hand to the front of my thigh before he slides two fingers inside me. I gasp and try to tell him that he does too, but I can't find the words as my body threatens to fly apart at the seams.

He's moving his fingers in and out, and I'm moving against him. I'm lost in the sensations and the darkness that's consuming me, and I'm not sure I'll ever find my way back.

I'm spiraling higher and higher, and I'm on the edge of something cataclysmic, ready to shatter.

"Maverick," I cry.

"Yes, my songbird," he whispers, his breath on my ear.

I'm about to say more, but then he slides his fingers from inside me.

I blink my eyes open, and I'm caught in the darkness of his gaze. I'm caught in the storm.

"You're perfect," he whispers.

His hand trails across my body, and I shudder beneath him. He hooks his fingers into the sides of my panties once more, and then he tugs.

I'm shaking beneath him, my naked body laid bare before him.

I close my eyes when I feel his hand against my thigh. I can feel his breath on my virgin flesh, and then his fingers are sliding through my wetness.

"I want to taste you, my songbird," he whispers.

The ache between my legs is unbearable. My entire body is screaming for something, and I feel like I'll die if I don't get it.

I whimper as I feel his tongue against my core, and that's it. I'm *breaking*.

I'm shattering into a million pieces beneath him, and I cry out as he licks me until the little aftershocks fade away.

I sag against the pillows and then slowly open my eyes. I can feel my cheeks burning from the intensity of my orgasm.

He's staring at me, the intensity on his face more powerful than ever before.

He's beautiful and dark, and I can feel a low, simmering desire rising up in me.

"Are you sure?" he asks.

I nod silently before I scramble to my knees and gasp as the sheer size of him towers before me.

I stroke my fingers lightly up and down his length. His head falls back as he groans deeply.

I lick my lips before I reach out and guide him into my mouth. He's hot and hard and silky soft at the same time.

"Fuck," he hisses as I swirl my tongue around the head of his cock.

I swirl my tongue around him tentatively and then

suck on the tip before I slide him deeper into my mouth.

I let his groans of pleasure guide me. The way his hands flex encourage me.

I'm so turned on, so desperate for this, and I moan around his cock as I take him deeper than ever before.

He reaches down and wraps his fingers in my hair, tugging.

"That's it, songbird," he murmurs. "Just like that."

The pressure against the back of my throat is intense, but I don't want him to stop. I want more. I want all of him.

I take everything he has to give and then some, and I can feel him grow even harder and thicker.

The pressure is so intense as he hits the back of my throat.

Suddenly he pulls on my hair with a growl as his cock slides from my mouth with a wet "plop."

"Have to have you. *Now*." His voice is dark and strangled as he positions himself between my legs.

He grabs the back of my neck, his eyes blazing into mine as he whispers, "You're mine, Willow. *Mine*."

With that, he plunges inside me. My back arches as he fills me completely, stretching me impossibly wide as he stakes his claim on my virginity, making me his completely.

I feel the burn, the fullness, and then he stills, letting me get used to the feel of him inside me before he pulls back slowly and then drives back inside me hard.

"That's right," he whispers just before his lips lock onto mine. "Sing for me little songbird."

And I do. I throw my head back and scream as I spasm around him, my orgasm on his cock harder than the one I had when he was going down on me.

I can feel my walls clenching around him, and he moans into my mouth as he comes inside me, his release flooding me until it's squirting out between us.

"Fuck, Willow," he groans as he holds me close to his chest and jerks inside me.

I didn't know my body could feel this way, and I never want to lose this.

I press myself into him, holding onto him just as closely as he is me until he collapses onto his side and rolls us so that I'm laying atop him.

He pets me, and I sigh like a contented cat as I fall asleep—safe—in his arms.

Willow

I WAKE SLOWLY, a smile spreading across my face. Maverick's arms are wrapped around me, his body pressed against my back. Last night was incredible. I've never felt so connected to someone. It's like our souls are intertwined. I want to wake up like this every morning, tangled in Maverick's strong embrace.

I carefully turn to face him, not wanting to disturb his sleep. His face looks so peaceful, his muscular chest rising and falling with each breath. I lightly trace my fingers across his tattooed bicep. A shiver runs through me as I remember how those arms held me so securely just hours ago. I feel safe with Maverick in a way I've never felt with anyone else before.

After a few minutes, Maverick's eyes flutter open. He gives me a sleepy smile. "Good morning, beautiful," he murmurs, pulling me closer. I melt into him, my lips finding his. The kiss deepens, our passion igniting once more.

A loud knock at the door breaks the moment. I groan in frustration. Maverick sighs, slowly untangling himself from me. "I'll get it. Stay here." I pout playfully as he pulls on his jeans.

After Maverick leaves, I stretch leisurely before climbing out of bed. As I walk to the bathroom, my foot kicks something on the floor. I glance down to see a white envelope. My name is scribbled across it in bold, black letters. Hands trembling, I pick it up and tear it open.

My blood turns to ice as I read the letter's contents. It's from Vincent. He knows intimate details about my schedule, my relationships, my innermost thoughts and fears. The letter is threatening, possessive, disturbing.

I sink to the floor, wrapping my arms around myself. How does he know so much about me? I feel exposed, vulnerable. Like he can see inside my mind. Tears spill down my cheeks.

In an instant, Maverick is by my side. "What

happened?" His voice is urgent. I wordlessly hand him the letter. As he reads, his jaw clenches, his eyes flashing with anger. "Fuck," he growls. He pulls me into his arms, holding me tightly. "I'm sorry, Willow, You weren't supposed to see this, little songbird."

I shake my head. "It's not your fault."

"You're safe, Willow. I won't let him hurt you." Maverick's voice is fierce yet gentle. I cling to him, sobbing into his chest. He doesn't say anything, just keeps stroking my hair, anchoring me.

After some time, my tears subside. I take a shaky breath, comforted by Maverick's steady presence. He tilts my chin up, gazing into my eyes. "I've got you, Willow. I promise you. I won't let him get near you."

I manage a small smile, reaching up to caress his stubbled cheek. "I know," I whisper. "I trust you." Maverick pulls me close again, his body warm and solid against mine.

"Come on," Maverick says after a time. He lifts me to my feet and guides me to the plush couch in the dimly lit living room. I sink into the soft leather, my body weary from crying. He sits close beside me, his thigh pressed against mine. I lean into him, seeking his warmth and strength.

His arm comes around me, hand gently stroking my shoulder. The contact is electric, sending little sparks across my skin. I glance up at him through my lashes. His eyes are dark, filled with an emotion I can't quite name. Desire? Concern? Both?

"Talk to me, Willow," he murmurs, his voice a low rumble.

I take a shaky breath, comforted by his nearness. "I just...I feel so violated. The thought of him watching me, following me..." I trail off with a shudder.

Maverick's jaw clenches, his hand tightening on my shoulder. "That bastard won't get near you again. I'll die before I let him touch you."

His vehemence startles me. I search his face, seeing the sincerity in his eyes. Slowly, I nod, some of the tension leaving my body. If anyone can protect me, it's Maverick.

We sit in silence for a moment. Then, unable to resist, I lean forward, brushing my lips against his. Maverick inhales sharply, then his mouth claims mine in a searing kiss. My fingers tangle in his hair as our tongues meet, hot and urgent.

His hands slide down my back, pressing me against his hard chest. I moan softly, every nerve ending igniting. In this moment, it's just us, all my fears fading away. Maverick makes me feel wanted, desired...safe. As long as I'm with him, nothing else matters.

Maverick's hands are like fire on my skin as they slip under my shirt, tracing up my spine. I shiver at his touch, heat pooling low in my belly. Our kisses grow more frantic, both of us consumed by need.

With a low growl, Maverick lifts me onto his lap so I'm straddling him. The evidence of his arousal presses insistently against my inner thigh. I rock my hips, eliciting a ragged groan from him. His fingers dig into my waist, hard enough to bruise. The thought sends a spike of arousal through me.

"Willow," he rasps, his voice strained. "We shouldn't..."

But his protest dies as I capture his mouth again, nibbling at his bottom lip. "I want you," I breathe against his skin.

That's all the encouragement he needs. Deftly, he flips me onto my back on the couch, coming over me like a wave. His stubble scrapes my neck as his lips blaze a trail down to my collarbone. I whimper, clutching at him desperately.

We come together in a clash of passion and heat, losing ourselves in each other. Maverick fills me, his powerful body moving with mine as pleasure crests and breaks over us again and again.

Afterward, I lay curled against him, utterly spent. His heart thuds steadily under my palm. I've never felt as safe, or as satisfied, as I do in this moment. And I know Maverick will do whatever it takes to keep me protected. With him by my side, no stalker can touch me.

Maverick's fingers comb gently through my hair as I lay with my head nestled on his shoulder. His steady breaths and the warmth of his body envelop me in a sense of comfort and security.

"I'm scared," I confess softly, tears pricking at my eyes. "What if he finds me again?"

Maverick's arm tightens around me. "I won't let him get anywhere near you," he says, his voice low but firm.

I glance up to meet his gaze. The intensity in his eyes makes my heart flutter.

"You can't know that for sure," I reply, hating the quaver in my voice.

Maverick brushes his thumb over my cheek, wiping away an escaped tear. "Yes, I can. I'm here with you now, and I'll keep staying with you, for as long as it takes. I promise."

His words thaw some of the icy fingers of fear gripping my chest. I manage a small smile. "Thank you. I'm glad I have you."

Maverick smiles back, a rare softness in his rugged features. He presses a kiss to my forehead.

We sit in silence for a few moments, drawing comfort from each other's presence. I focus on the steadiness of his breathing, the strength of his embrace.

I lift my head from Maverick's shoulder, my eyes searching his. There's a new intensity in his gaze that makes my pulse quicken. His eyes flick down to my lips, then back up to meet my stare.

Slowly, he reaches out, brushing back a lock of hair that has fallen across my cheek. His fingertips linger, tracing along my jawline. I shiver at his touch, electricity skittering across my skin.

I lean into him, tilting my chin up in invitation. Maverick's eyes darken, his desire evident. He slides his hand around to cradle the back of my neck, his fingers threading up into my hair.

Our lips meet, soft and seeking at first. Then the kiss deepens. I clutch at his shoulders, melting against him. Maverick pulls me closer, one hand pressed against the small of my back.

We come up for air, foreheads touching, breathing ragged. I trail my fingers down his chest, feeling the rapid pounding of his heart.

"Will it always be like this?" I whisper. "Will we always want each other this way?"

Slowly he nods, his hand coming up to cup my cheek. "Always," he murmurs. "I'll always want you, my little songbird."

Our mouths find each other again, the rest of the world fading away.

But then Maverick breaks the kiss, pulling back just

enough to meet my gaze. His eyes are conflicted, brow furrowed. I can sense the internal war raging within him.

"Willow..." he begins, then trails off with a heavy sigh.

My fingertips trace the stubble along his jaw. "What is it?" I ask softly.

He closes his eyes briefly, leaning into my touch. When he opens them again, I see resignation.

"This...us...it's complicated," he says. "I have a job to do. I can't let my feelings get in the way of protecting you."

I nod, swallowing down the lump in my throat. I understand, but it still hurts.

"I know," I whisper.

We sit in loaded silence for several heartbeats. I can feel Maverick's inner turmoil, his desire and duty warring within. My own heart aches with want and uncertainty.

Finally, Maverick takes my hand, his thumb stroking over my knuckles.

"But when I'm with you like this...none of that seems to matter," he admits.

I meet his gaze again, seeing warmth and tenderness there now.

"I need you to know I've never felt about anyone the way I feel about you."

Tears prick at my eyes. I lace my fingers through his, squeezing gently.

"Me too," I tell him.

We come together once more, mouths meeting in a soft, lingering kiss. No more words are needed.

Maverick's hand comes up to cradle my face as our kiss deepens, no longer soft but hungry and demanding. The air between us ignites with pent up longing. It doesn't matter that he took me just a few moments ago. I need him again already.

My fingers twist into his shirt, pulling him against me.

Our breaths mingle in heated pants and gasps as we paw at each other. The cool air raises goosebumps on my bare skin, but Maverick's touch soon warms me. His hands blaze trails down my sides, over my hips, leaving no inch of me unexplored.

I meet his passion equally, nails raking down the muscular plane of his back, eliciting a low groan. We are beyond reason now, our bodies taking over in primal communication.

Maverick lifts me effortlessly, laying me back on the plush leather couch. The contrast of soft and hard heightens every sensation. He settles over me, strong and solid. Our eyes lock and an unspoken question passes between us. I answer by wrapping my legs around his waist.

We both cry out as he enters me in one smooth stroke. The feeling of connection is even more intense than our first time. I cling to him desperately, wanting more of him, all of him.

"Fuck, Willow, you'll be the death of me, beautiful," he groans as he buries his face in my neck and begins to plunge into me harder.

I throw my hips up at him, fucking him back, welcoming him with each powerful thrust of his body.

We move together in perfect sync, chasing the crest of ecstasy.

Higher and higher we climb until finally release takes us. Crying out his name, I shatter around him. Maverick buries his face in my hair, groaning as he follows me over the edge.

We remain tangled up long afterward, our hearts gradually slowing, breaths evening out. No words yet, just hands lazily caressing slick skin.

Whatever comes next, we have this moment. I want to live in it forever.

CHAPTER
NINE

Maverick

I NOD to the doorman as I enter Willow's building, hyper-alert as always. Ever since Willow gave herself to me, it's been hell being away from her. I don't leave her much—only when I have to. Most nights now, I stay with her in her room, but I had to get to my office today.

And I was miserable every second I was away from her. I want to live with my cock permanently inside her. She consumes my every thought, and I feel like a drug addict jonesing for another hit every second that I'm away from her.

I crave her like I've never craved anything in my

motherfucking life, and my cock is already getting hard knowing that I'm on my way back to her.

In the elevator, I review the plan for her event tonight, contingencies spinning through my mind. When the doors open, I step out and freeze.

Her apartment door hangs open.

Icy fear grips me. My mouth goes dry, and my throat tightens.

In an instant I'm sprinting down the hall, heart pounding. I burst into the apartment, gun drawn. "Willow?"

No answer. The place is in shambles—furniture overturned, glass shattered across the floor. Signs of a struggle.

I sweep each room, fear rising. No sign of her. As I step back into the living room, my boot crunches on something. A black rose, petals crushed and torn.

Rage wells up inside me, white-hot.

I failed her.

But I won't rest until she's safe.

Vincent Barnes, you messed with the wrong girl.

I'll scour the city if I must, uncover every dark corner until I find the monster who took her. And then, I'll make him regret ever touching her.

Jaw set, I stride out the door. *I'm coming for you, Willow. Just hold on a little longer.*

This ends *tonight*.

TEN

Willow

I'M ALONE in my apartment, curtains drawn, doors locked. But the prickling on my neck tells me I'm being watched. My heart races as I peer through the blinds into the dark night below. A shadowy figure stands under the streetlamp, face obscured.

My phone buzzes, an unknown number. With trembling hands, I answer.

"Hello, Willow," an icy voice slithers through the speaker. "You look so beautiful tonight. That little black dress is just perfect."

I gasp, peering down at my attire. How does he know what I'm wearing?

"Surprised? You shouldn't be. I've been watching you, my dear. I know your every move."

"What do you want from me?" I ask, my voice quivering.

"All in good time, my sweet."

The line goes dead, his bone-chilling words lingering. I drop the phone, hands clasped over my hammering heart.

My breath catches as I hear a faint scratching at the door.

He's here.

Vincent found me.

I spring into action, adrenaline pumping through my veins. My only chance is to run. The scratching grows louder as I race to the window and wrench it open.

The fire escape looms below me, rusted metal steps leading down into the dark alley. I sling my leg over the sill, glancing back as the apartment door splinters open. Vincent's hulking form fills the doorway, eyes glinting.

"Leaving so soon, my pet? The fun hasn't even started," he purrs.

I scream as he lunges, just barely slipping from his grasp. My feet hit the fire escape, and I'm flying down the steps. Vincent's thunderous footsteps echo above me as I leap to the ground.

The alley swallows me into darkness. I run blindly, my heels clicking on the pavement. Have to get away, have to escape.

But his voice drifts through the shadows, seeming to come from every direction at once.

"You can't hide, Willow. I'll always find you..."

I burst out of the alley onto the empty street, the glow of the streetlights my only guide. My lungs burn as I sprint down the sidewalk, my hair whipping behind me. I dare a glance back, my heart seizing when I see Vincent's hulking form in pursuit.

He's gaining on me. I veer left, scrambling through a gap in a chainlink fence into a vacant construction site. The half-built frames of houses and skeletal beams loom like monsters in the dark. I weave between them, praying for somewhere to hide.

Vincent's heavy footsteps echo closer. "Why run, my pet? Don't you want to play?" His voice seems to come from everywhere at once, taunting me.

I spot a bulldozer and crawl underneath it, tucking myself into the shadows. My pulse thunders in my ears.

Go away, just go away!

Crunching footsteps circle the dozer. I clamp a hand over my mouth, tears streaming down my face. Suddenly, Vincent's upside-down face appears as he crouches to peer under the dozer.

"There you are. Found you."

I scream as he grabs my ankles and drags me out. I kick and claw at the dirt, but his grip is iron. He flips me onto my back, straddling me. I beat against his chest, but he pins my wrists above my head. His face looms over mine, his eyes cold yet hungry.

"Shhh, don't fight. You're only making this more difficult for yourself..."

I spit in his face. "Go to hell!"

He slaps me—hard. My vision spins. "Hell is where I'll take you if you don't behave!" he hisses.

I won't let it end like this. As he moves to grab me, I bring my knee up hard. He howls in pain, his grip loosening. I punch his throat and scramble away, fleeing once more into the dark labyrinth of beams.

His enraged roar pursues me. "You can't escape me, Willow!"

But I can try.

"Maverick!" I scream the only name that comes to mind as loud as I can, so loudly that my lungs hurt.

Please! Save me!

Maverick

WILLOW'S SCREAM pierces the night air. My blood turns to ice as her cry echoes down the dark alley. I break into a sprint, my shoes pounding against the pavement. Fear courses through my veins, but determination fuels my muscles. I will not fail her.

The alley stretches before me, shrouded in shadow. I strain my ears for any sound of Willow's struggle, for any hint of her location. Only the frantic beat of my heart fills my ears.

Come on, Willow, call out again. Let me find you.

Ahead, a grunt and the sound of a scuffle. My fists

clench and I pour on the speed. Nobody hurts my girl and gets away with it. Rounding the corner, I see them. Willow on the ground, her wrists bound. A dark figure looming over her. Rage erupts within me, hot and violent.

In three long strides I'm on him, my shoulder slamming into his torso. We crash into the brick wall, and he lets out a gasp. I pin him in place, my forearm crushing his windpipe.

Cold blue eyes meet mine.

Vincent.

"You chose the wrong girl to mess with," I growl. His lips curl into a smirk even as he chokes for breath. My vision goes red. I haul back and smash my fist into his face. Once, twice, three times. Blood spurts from his nose, but still he grins through split lips.

"She's mine now," he gurgles, blood bubbling on his lips. "You can't stop what's coming for her."

I snarl and knee him hard in the gut. He doubles over wheezing. In one smooth motion, I flip him around and wrench his arms behind his back.

"She belongs to no one," I hiss in his ear. With a snap, I dislocate his shoulder. Vincent screams. I let his body drop to the filthy concrete. He won't be giving us any more trouble tonight.

I rush to Willow's side. As I cut her bonds, our eyes meet. Relief and something deeper shine in her emerald gaze. I cup her cheek, wiping away a smudge of dirt. She's safe. I won't let anyone hurt my songbird ever again. This I vow.

Her eyes shine with wonder as she takes in the scene before her. Vincent lies crumpled and bloodied on the alley floor, groaning in pain. I stand over him, fists clenched, breathing hard.

"Maverick..." she whispers.

"It's okay. You're safe now."

I help her up, steadying her as she finds her feet. She stumbles into me and I catch her, holding her close. Her body trembles against mine.

"Shh, it's over," I murmur, stroking her hair.

She looks up at me, eyes wide. "How did you do that? You were so fast, so strong..."

I give a small smile. "It's my job to protect you."

Her hands curl into my shirt, gripping tight. We stay that way for a moment, her finding comfort in my embrace. I breathe in the floral scent of her shampoo, letting it soothe my raging nerves. She's here. She's safe.

Finally I pull back, brushing a stray curl behind her ear. "Let's get you out of here."

I keep an arm around her as I guide her from that dark alley. I radio my men, and they have the cops come apprehend the fucker.

Willow presses close, still shaken. But the tremors slowly subside as we leave that place behind.

As we reach the car, Willow turns to me, her eyes filled with emotion. "I was so scared tonight. But you saved me."

She steps closer, her hands coming to rest on my chest. My heart pounds against her palm.

"I don't know what I'd do without you," she whispers.

Her lips part slightly as she gazes up at me. Unable to resist, I bring my hand to her cheek, caressing it gently. She leans into my touch, eyelids fluttering closed.

Slowly, I lower my head until our lips meet in a soft, tentative kiss. Willow melts against me, her body molding to mine. The kiss deepens, our suppressed passion finally finding release.

I've never wanted anything as much as I want her in this moment. My fierce, beautiful songbird. I vow now to never let her go. To stay by her side and keep her safe, no matter the cost.

We break apart, breathless. Willow's eyes shine like emeralds as she smiles up at me.

"I love you," she whispers.

My heart swells. "I love you too. With everything that I am."

I pull her close once more, more determined than ever to never let this precious girl out of my sight again. She is my light, my reason for being. And I will move heaven and earth to protect her.

Always.

EPILOGUE

Willow

MY HEART THUDS against my ribs as Maverick's piercing blue eyes meet mine. We sit facing each other on the plush hotel sofa, our knees nearly touching.

"I don't know how to thank you for everything you've done for me," I say, my voice low and earnest. "You've been my rock this past year. My protector."

Maverick reaches across the narrow space between us and takes my hand in his. "It's been my privilege to keep you safe, Willow. But you're not a job to me anymore. You haven't been for a long time."

His thumb traces slow circles over my knuckles. I shiver, desire coiling hot and low in my belly. We've been dancing around this for months, neither brave enough to cross the line between client and bodyguard. But that line has blurred beyond recognition.

"I want to be with you," I whisper. "As partners. In all things."

Maverick's eyes darken, his grip on my hand tightening. "I'll always protect you, Willow. Nothing will change that. We'll face the future together."

My heart swells. This formidable man has seen me at my most vulnerable, yet he looks at me now with such tenderness. I lean in close, breathing him in, willing him to close the distance between us.

Maverick's breath catches as I press closer, our lips just inches apart.

"This won't be easy," he says, his voice rough. "Your life is complicated. Dangerous. There are more Vincents out there. Freaks who would become obsessed with you."

I brush my fingers along his stubbled jaw. "I know. But I'm not afraid, not with you by my side."

Maverick closes his eyes briefly, a pained expression flickering across his face. When he opens them again, I see a tempest of emotion in those blue depths.

"I'll never stop protecting you. No matter what comes at us, I swear it. You are my everything, Willow. I hope you know that. I am obsessed with you."

His solemn vow sends a shiver down my spine. I

know he means every word. Maverick has never let me down before.

I smile softly. "Then I have nothing to fear. As long as we're together, we can weather any storm."

Maverick's eyes blaze as he finally eliminates the space between us. His lips capture mine in a searing kiss that steals my breath away. My fingers twist in his shirt, pulling him against me.

We come together like two flames merging into an inferno, desperate and urgent. I pour all my love and trust into our kiss. Maverick answers with a possessive passion that brands me as his.

I pull back slightly, catching my breath as I gaze up at Maverick. His eyes are dark with desire, but there's a vulnerability there too. This man has given everything to keep me safe, and now our relationship is changing.

"I know you'll always protect me," I say softly. "But I want more than that. I want to share my dreams with you, my hopes for the future."

Maverick nods, his expression serious. "I want that too. I've spent my whole life being a shield, keeping people at a distance. With you, I feel like I could be more."

He takes my hands in his larger ones. "Tell me about your dreams, Willow. I want to know what's in your heart."

I smile, feeling a rush of excitement. "My music is

so important to me. I want my songs to reach people, to move them. And I want to perform all over the world, see new places and share my gift."

I meet his gaze. "With you by my side, I know I can make it happen. You give me the courage to reach for more."

Maverick squeezes my hands. "You have an amazing talent. I'll do everything I can to help your star rise. Your dreams are mine now too."

He pauses, seeming to gather his courage. "You've given me something I didn't think I'd ever have. A real purpose, beyond just surviving. I want to build a life with you, Willow."

My heart swells with emotion. We seal our vows with a long, sweet kiss, our future unfolding before us like an open road.

Maverick's hands slide down to my hips, pulling me against him. Our kiss deepens, fueled by longing. I run my fingers through his hair, thrilling at his touch.

He lifts me effortlessly, laying me down on the couch beneath him. My skin tingles everywhere his hands explore. We shed our clothes piece by piece, our breathing ragged.

"I need you, Willow," he rasps, his body hard against mine. "I've never wanted anyone the way I want you."

"Then take me," I whisper. "I'm yours."

We come together in a blaze of passion. His hands and mouth claim my skin with sensual purpose. I arch into him, dizzy with desire, craving more of his addictive touch.

We move as one, our gasps and moans mingling. The world falls away until there is only Maverick surrounding me, possessing me. I give myself to him completely, caught in the storm of sensation.

Afterward, we lie entwined, floating in bliss. I trace the scars on his body, testaments to his sacrifices. He cradles me close, surrounding me with his strength. Our hearts thudding in tandem. Maverick kisses my hair, his voice rough with emotion. "I love you, Willow. I'll never leave your side."

I smile against his chest, feeling safe in the circle of his arms. "I love you too. Always."

Maverick tilts my chin up, his eyes boring into mine. "I vow to you, Willow, I will always be by your side. As your lover, confidant, and protector." His voice drops lower. "I will shield you from all harm, cherish you above all others, and give you my full devotion."

My breath catches at the intensity of his words. This powerful, enigmatic man offering everything he is.

I press closer, heart swelling. "I vow the same to you, Maverick. I am yours, now and forever."

Our lips meet in a searing kiss, a promise sealed. No matter what the future brings, I know our bond is unbreakable. We've found our missing piece in each other.

I snuggle into his embrace, perfectly content. The future is ours for the taking. With Maverick as my partner, my love, my everything, I know we can weather any storm.

This is just the beginning for us. And I can't wait to turn the page.

Want a free book? Go to www.authoremmabray.com.

9 798822 399662 0